Are there forests in the clouds?

Written by Tom Ottway

Illustrated by Alice Negri

Collins

What's in this book?

Listen and say

elephant

snake

parrot

frog

Download the audio at www.collins.co.uk/839674

sunny

clouds

crocodile

forest

monkey

sloth

3 participants

Kissa

Victor

Sam

Victor: I'm Victor. I live here.

 Sam: I'm Sam. Wow! Do you live in the clouds?

 Victor: No, I live in a forest.

 Kissa: I'm Kissa. I live in a forest, too.
Are there forests in the clouds?

Victor: This is the cloud forest. These forests always have clouds.

 Kissa: Always?

 Victor: Yes, it's good. The clouds make a lot of water. People and animals need water.

 Kissa:

 Sam:

Sam: Are there any animals in the cloud forest?

 Victor: Yes. The trees in this forest grow tall with all the water. Tall trees are good for the animals. They can hide in them and they can drink the water – like the snake in this photo. Can you see it?

3 participants

 Victor: You can see bears, monkeys, snakes and birds.

 Kissa: Wow! Look at the colours on those birds! What are they?

 Victor: Those are parrots.

 Sam: And what's that at the top of the tree?

 Victor: It's a very beautiful but slow animal. A sloth! It's sleeping. Sloths sleep a lot.

 Kissa: It's so pretty!

3 participants

 Kissa: Let me show you my forest! I live in the Bwindi forest. It's a beautiful forest.

 Victor: It's very dark! Is it always dark?

 Kissa: Yes. There are a lot of trees so you can't see the sun.

 Sam: Those butterflies are fantastic!

Kissa: You can walk in the forest and see many things.
Look at the elephants in this photo.

Sam: Wow! 😃 And can you see the baby playing with its mother? ♥

Victor: Show us your forest, Sam. 😃

 Sam: This is my forest.
It's the Daintree forest.
It's often hot and
wet here.

 Victor: Is it hot and
wet today?

 Sam: Yes, today it's wet
and sunny.

 Kissa: There's a lot of water!

 Sam: Yes, there is. You can
see animals in the
forest here, too. There
are beautiful green
frogs and snakes in
the trees.

 Victor: I can see them.

 Sam: There are rivers in the forest. But we need to be careful next to the river because there are crocodiles.

 Kissa: Look! You can see two.

 Victor: They're big!

 Kissa: Look at those teeth!

 Sam: Yes. It's not safe to swim in the rivers.

 Victor: Oh!

 Sam: This is Cape Tribulation.

 Kissa: And is that the Daintree forest?

 Sam: Yes. The rivers in the forest go to the sea. You can see where the forest ends and the beach starts.

 Kissa:

 Victor: I didn't know that forests could be so different.

 Kissa: I didn't know there were forests in the clouds!

Picture dictionary

Listen and repeat

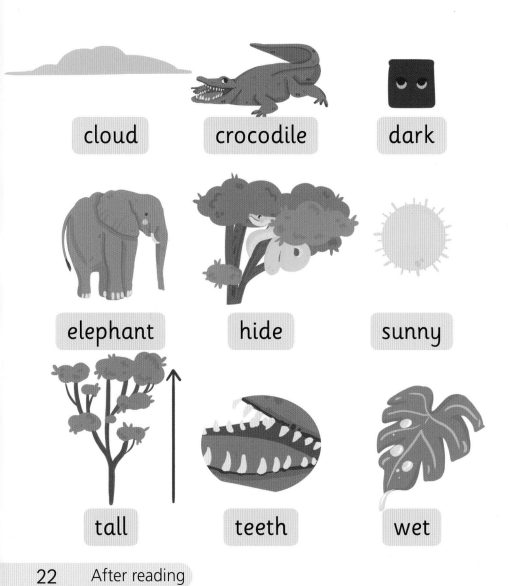

cloud

crocodile

dark

elephant

hide

sunny

tall

teeth

wet

1 Look and say "*Yes*" or "*No*"

2 Listen and say

Collins

Published by Collins
An imprint of HarperCollins*Publishers*
Westerhill Road
Bishopbriggs
Glasgow
G64 2QT

HarperCollins*Publishers*
1st Floor, Watermarque Building
Ringsend Road
Dublin 4
Ireland

William Collins' dream of knowledge for all began with the publication of his first book in 1819.

A self-educated mill worker, he not only enriched millions of lives, but also founded a flourishing publishing house. Today, staying true to this spirit, Collins books are packed with inspiration, innovation and practical expertise. They place you at the centre of a world of possibility and give you exactly what you need to explore it.

© HarperCollins*Publishers* Limited 2020

10 9 8 7 6 5 4 3 2

ISBN 978-0-00-839674-9

Collins® and COBUILD® are registered trademarks of HarperCollins*Publishers* Limited

www.collins.co.uk/elt

British Library Cataloguing in Publication Data

A catalogue record for this publication is available from the British Library.

Author: Tom Ottway
Illustrator: Alice Negri (Beehive)
Series editor: Rebecca Adlard
Commissioning editor: Fiona Undrill and Zoë Clarke
Publishing manager: Lisa Todd
Product managers: Jennifer Hall and Caroline Green
In-house editor: Alma Puts Keren
Project manager: Emily Hooton
Editor: Frances Amrani
Proofreaders: Natalie Murray and Michael Lamb
Cover designer: Kevin Robbins
Typesetter: 2Hoots Publishing Services Ltd
Audio produced by id audio, London
Reading guide author: Emma Wilkinson
Production controller: Rachel Weaver
Printed and bound by: GPS Group, Slovenia

MIX
Paper from responsible sources

FSC
www.fsc.org

FSC™ C007454

Download the audio for this book and a reading guide for parents and teachers at www.collins.co.uk/839674